The Happy Easter Book

by JOSIE JONES

illustrated by JOHN NEZ

A GOLDEN BOOK • NEW YORK

Western Publishing Company, Inc., Racine, Wisconsin 53404

It's nearly Easter!
At school, Ryan draws a picture of the Easter bunny. Martha makes a little basket out of paper.

At the end of the day, the teacher reads an
Easter poem and then passes out candy eggs.

The next morning, Ryan and Martha go to the store with Mother. They buy an Easter egg color kit.

When they get home, Ryan asks, "When can we color the eggs?"
"Right now!" says Mother.

First, Mother puts the eggs on the stove to cook. Ryan sets the timer.

When the eggs are done, Mother puts them in a pan of water to cool.

Martha drops little colored tablets into bowls of warm water. The tablets melt and color the water.

Martha dips an egg into the red water. After a few minutes, she lifts out a beautiful red egg.

Ryan slips some eggs into the purple water, then some into the yellow water.

All the eggs are colored.
With a special marking pen, Ryan writes
his name on a blue egg. Martha paints a
face on a pink egg.

Just then, Grandma and Grandpa arrive.
"The eggs look so pretty!" says Grandma.

Grandpa takes Ryan and Martha to the candy store for a special Easter treat.

Ryan chooses a chocolate bunny. Martha decides on jelly beans.

At home, Martha tries on the dress that Mother made for her. She is going to wear it in the Easter parade.

Grandma is decorating the Easter bonnet that she is going to wear in the parade.

Father reads a bedtime story. The children fall asleep and dream about what the Easter bunny is going to bring them.

Does the Easter bunny come? Yes, he does!
He brings Easter baskets for Ryan and
Martha, and he hides eggs for them to find.

In the morning, Ryan and Martha run downstairs and see the baskets filled with Easter treats. Martha spies a tiny toy lamb tucked in her basket.

They go outside to hunt for eggs. Martha sees one beside a tree. Ryan finds two eggs in a bed of daffodils.

Soon they find all the eggs.

It is time for the Easter parade. Everybody gets all dressed up. Grandma puts on her bonnet.

Grandma wins the prize for the fanciest hat in the parade!
Happy Easter, everyone!